Raintree is an imprint of Capstone Global Library Limited, a company incorporated in England and Wales having its registered office at 264 Banbury Road, Oxford, OX2 7DY – Registered company number: 6695582

www.raintree.co.uk
myorders@raintree.co.uk

ISBN 978 1 4747 6716 3
22 21 20 19 18
10 9 8 7 6 5 4 3 2 1

British Library Cataloguing in Publication Data
A full catalogue record for this book is available from the British Library.

All characters in this publication are fictitious and any resemblance to real persons, living or dead, is purely coincidental.

Printed and bound in India

in
Zero Gravity

Ailsa Wild

with illustrations by
BEN WOOD

raintree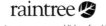

a Capstone company — publishers for children

For Beatrice and Arlen. I know you're too grown up for Squishy, but I wanted you to have this one anyway.
Love from your fairy gold-mother.
– Ailsa

For Dad! Happy retirement!
– Ben

Chapter One

"**Bzzzt!**" I say. "This is Squishy Taylor, exiting the space station. Over."

I swing myself out of the airlock door towards the meteor damage. The space station is broken, and my legs float away from me as I hold tight. I'm hanging here in zero gravity. My life is in danger. If I let go now, I'll go drifting into deep space, just a spinning white dot in a dark universe.

"*Bzzzt.* Roger that, Squishy. Ground control on standby. Over," Vee says, because she's ground control.

"*Bzzzt*," I say. "Meteor damage is worse than we thought. I'll need to be here for a while." I look closely at the red paint, my legs dangling into space.

Vee's voice changes. "Squishy, that's not fair. It's supposed to be *my* turn doing space station repairs." She's stopped pretending to speak into the microphone. She's standing on the woodchips, frowning at me, while I swing across the monkey bars.

We're at the playground near our apartment. Our playground is extra cool because it has an actual pretend space station at one end of the monkey bars.

Some people in orange vests with a truck came a few weeks ago and attached it. Just off the woodchips, they also put in a whole solar system you can turn with a handle. The sun is taller than my dad.

"You're breaking up, ground control," I say. "I can't hear you."

"*Squishy.*" Vee sounds a bit grumpy.

"I'm not getting any sound," I say, pretending to fiddle with my earpiece. "Maybe the moon has come between us."

Vee's twin, Jessie, laughs out loud. She's been turning the solar system really slowly, watching the orbit patterns, but now she looks at us. "The moon can't get between Earth and a space station, you **dumbo**," she says.

Jessie and Vee are my bonus sisters. They are the bonus I got when I moved in with my dad and their mum. Except sometimes Jessie and Vee *aren't* a bonus, like now. They're annoying.

"Squishy, it's *my* turn," Vee says.

I swing myself up to sit on top of the monkey bars. I kick my feet, not wanting to come down.

"Do you *know* how far away the moon is?" Jessie says, coming to stand below me. "It's two hundred and thirty-eight *thousand*, nine hundred miles away."

Jessie likes astronomy, and she likes facts. So of course she knows this.

"And do you know how far away the space station is?" Jessie doesn't wait for an answer. "Two hundred and forty-nine miles away," she says, looking super pleased with herself. "So there's no way the moon comes between Earth and the space station."

I do a **roll-back-flip** to the ground and stand in front of them. There's something seriously suspicious about Jessie's facts.

"That's not true," I say. "The space station *can't* be only two hundred and forty-nine miles away."

"Fine, we'll Google it when we get home." Jessie loves Googling things to prove she's right. But this time I know she's wrong.

"Jessie, Mum told me that it's four hundred and sixty miles between

London and Geneva. How can the space station be closer than England is to Switzerland?"

We stare at each other.

"Squishy," Jessie says, her eyes widening, "the space station *is actually* closer than London is to Geneva. That is the **coolest thing ever**."

She's so surprised that I almost believe her. We all laugh, and it makes us forget to argue any more.

Vee has an idea. "Let's do astronaut training," she says. "Then no one has to be ground control."

Astronauts need to be really fit, so we've made up our own astronaut training routine. It's mostly chin-ups, jumps and special flips off the monkey bars. They're things we already know, but the rule is you have to do them really fast and all in the right order.

"OK. I think I'll just . . . ," Jessie says, and heads back to the solar system.

Vee and I jump to the monkey bars together. We do chin-ups. One. Two. Then we swing our legs up and under. Hang from our knees. Swing our bodies. One. Two. Aaaand flip off.

We land on our feet and laugh.

"Now, jumps," we say together, because we both know the astronaut training order. We run to the steps and jump them. Jump up, up, up. Jump down, down, down. We're puffing and laughing and racing each other. Chin-ups again. My arms hurt. Hang from knees. Swing.

But my knees aren't gripping the bar as usual. I'm slipping. I'm falling! I'm going to land on my head.

I twist myself around in the air. Get my head up and my arms out and land – **thump!**

On my tummy. On the woodchips.

Ow. I can't breathe. It's like my lungs are broken.

I feel that thump crashing through my body, even though it's over. I can't breathe. **Maybe I'm dead**.

Then I gasp, so hard it hurts the back of my throat. My hands start stinging. My knees start hurting. My eyes are three centimetres away from the woodchips.

"Squishy, are you OK?" I can feel Vee leaning over me. Jessie runs over from the bench, and the toes of her trainers arrive at the woodchips where I'm staring.

"I want to go home," I whisper.

Chapter Two

Usually I don't care when I hurt myself. I'm not one of those kids who cries and needs a treat after every tiny, **ouchy** thing. But that thump was *hard*. My knees and hands hurt, and I feel a bit shaky. I walk between Jessie and Vee along the pavement to our apartment.

I can feel Jessie and Vee looking at me, like they're really worried, but I don't look at them. I'm biting my lip, and I've got a big lump in my throat. I don't cry in front of my bonus sisters.

Jessie puts her hand on my back, trying to comfort me. But her hand feels shy.

What I really want is a big, warm hug from my mum or dad.

We finally reach our apartment building and get the lift up to the eleventh floor, where we live.

Vee pushes into the kitchen first. "Squishy fell off the space station," she announces.

Dad isn't at home.

My whole stomach drops. I forgot. It's too early for Dad to be home on Tuesday. Alice, Jessie and Vee's mum, is sitting at the table with a pile of paper and a laptop. I don't hug Alice. I only just started living with her a few months ago.

Alice keeps typing and doesn't look up.

"It was bad," Vee says. "Like, **bang!**" She smashes her hands together, as if one hand is me and the other is the ground.

"Shhh," Alice says. "Baby's asleep." Baby belongs to Alice and Dad, so he's a brother to all of us equally.

"But Mum," Jessie says, "Squishy's bleeding."

Alice pushes her laptop away. "All right, **Squisho**, let's have a look at you."

I don't want her to look at me. I want Dad to be here hugging me.

"Can I Skype with Mum?" I ask. I'm trying not to cry.

Mum moved to Geneva, Switzerland, for nine months to work for the United Nations. That's why I live with Dad. I Skype Mum every day, but it's not the same as living in the same house as her.

Alice takes my hand, turning it over to look at the scrapes. "Let's clean this up before you Skype Devika."

Alice pulls out antiseptic and cotton wool balls and a bowl of warm water.

"Her knees are scraped up too," Jessie says.

I want to tell them I don't care about the scrapes. They're nothing, really. I just care about the feeling of the big thump when I landed. But if I talk, I'll cry.

I feel strange. Alice is nice, but I don't know her well enough. I watch her dab

the blood off my knee and miss my mum's soft cheek right next to mine.

When Alice has finished, she smiles at me and says, "Well done, sweetie. Do you need a hug?" She's never called me *sweetie* before. I look at her open arms and shake my head. She's only being nice because she's supposed to. I want my mum.

Finally Alice gives me the iPad, and I run to my bed with it. They tried to make us only use the iPad in the living room, but that didn't last long. I tap to open Skype.

"Hey, Squisho," Mum says. "What's happening?" She's at her desk at work because it's the start of the day in Geneva. Then she sees my **about-to-cry face** and leans in. "Oh, Squishy-sweet, what's wrong?"

My tears come out, hot and throat-achy. "I fell," I sob, "off the monkey bars."

"Oh, honey," she says.

"It was a really big thump," I say, "and then I couldn't breathe."

"It sounds like you got the wind knocked out of you," Mum says in just the right tone. She doesn't sound very worried, but she loves me a lot. I just want to snuggle into her. That's when I realize something. You can't hug over Skype. It makes me cry even harder.

"Hey," Mum says, after a while. "Isn't that meteor shower tonight?"

The meteor shower! I'd forgotten about that. We've been talking about it all week.

"What's the plan?" she asks.

My crying stops, and I feel myself starting to smile. "The building people gave Dad a rooftop key this morning," I say.

"**Woohoo!**" Mum cheers.

The building people almost said no to us going on the roof. Dad and Alice said we weren't allowed to pick the lock either, even though we know how. But they did try really hard to get the key. And finally, yesterday, the building people said yes.

"We're taking the telescope, and we're allowed to stay up until *ten o'clock*," I say.

Mum has a special mischievous face for when rules get broken. She used to be a bit of a **rebel**, and she still thinks breaking rules is fun. As long as they don't get broken too badly.

Mum grins. "Ten o'clock," she says, with her mischievous face on. "No way!"

"I know," I say. "On a school night!"

Mum laughs. "And I'm on a workday. So I should go, Squisho. Big hugs."

She hangs up, and my smile doesn't last long. I start to remember how hard I fell. That *thump* was ginormous.

Chapter Three

At nine o'clock, Alice and Baby go to bed. I don't. And neither do my bonus sisters.

We're watching *Lightspeed Kids* again while we wait. *Lightspeed Kids* is the best. It's the film that made me and Vee obsessed with being astronauts in the first place. Jessie was already obsessed with astronomy.

"All right, kids," Dad says. "Shoes and coats on. Let's go."

Jessie has packed the telescope neatly in its case and folded the tripod up small. We slide our shoes on and pull our coats on over our pyjamas.

Dad takes out the rooftop keys and waves them like a prize. We all troop out the door.

There's one more floor above ours, and after that, it's the roof. Dad leads the way up. The last stairs are more like a ladder. They're metal and steep. They also have a special gate on them to stop people from getting out. (Not that it can stop me or Vee. We are super ninja-climbers and have got over it twice already. Easy.) After that, there's a door.

And after that, the sky.

I follow Dad out onto the roof.

"Woooo!" I call. The big night makes me want to cheer and spin in circles. The city is **electric-sparkly** around us, reaching up towards the stars. The sky is completely clear. Vee spins with me, yodelling. Dad laughs. Jessie sets up the telescope, opening the tripod and lengthening all its legs.

Then the meteor shower starts.

It's like seeing fifty shooting stars all at once. Jessie's watching through the telescope.

"Amazing!" Dad says. He's got his arm around me, and we're both tipping our heads back.

The meteors just keep on falling.

"My turn! My turn!" Vee says, jiggling Jessie's elbow.

Jessie moves aside and comes over to me. "The telescope isn't that good anyway," she says.

"Hey, where are the meteors?" Vee says, squinting into it. "I can't see them."

"Yeah," Jessie says. "They move too fast, so there's no time to focus. Better without the telescope."

Dad lies down on his back, and I lie next to him on the hard concrete, looking up. My head leans on his warm shoulder. The meteors zoom across the sky. It's like watching **magic**. Only it's better than magic because it's real. It makes my heart thump and my mind feel calm.

"Imagine being out there, floating in space," I say. "**Zero gravity**." It's so hard to imagine being somewhere there's no down.

"It's not *zero* gravity," Jessie says, in her know-it-all voice. "It's microgravity."

I groan, and Vee laughs.

"But 'zero gravity' sounds so much cooler," Vee says. So I don't care about being corrected.

Vee wanders away from the telescope. Jessie has another turn, trying to focus it on Mars. I snuggle in closer to Dad.

Vee's voice comes from the other side of the roof. "Hey, cool! Come and look at this."

She sounds excited. When Vee uses that voice, there's usually an adventure on its way.

"Squishy, come and look!" Vee calls.

I leave Dad looking up at the stars, and Jessie trying to focus the telescope, and walk over to Vee.

She's peering out, with her elbows on the wall that goes all around the edge of the roof. "Look," she says, and points.

Opposite us is the really tall building where Boring Lady works. We always see her typing from our bedroom window. Next to it there's a building that's close to the same height as ours. That's where Vee is looking. Because on the roof of that building, somebody is moving around.

"Probably watching the meteors, like us," I say.

"No, *look*," Vee says.

I squint. The person is far away and it's hard to see, but it seems like they're wearing a space helmet. A dark one with a window over their face.

"It's practically midnight," I whisper. "Why is there an astronaut on the roof?"

The astronaut is standing next to something tall and cylindrical and pointed. **Something rocket-shaped?** I squeeze Vee's arm. The astronaut hoists something up into their arms and leans over. Then there's a massive shower of sparks. Bright white sparks, flying off the astronaut and up into the night.

"**Whoa!**" Vee and I say at once.

We lean against the wall, trying to work out what's going on, but it's

too dark. All we can see is sparks. Finally the sparks stop, and the astronaut pulls off her helmet. It's a woman with lots of red curly hair. She shakes her hair back off her face and leans towards her rocket. Is it *really* a rocket?

I can't believe we were playing astronauts, and now there's one in *real life*.

"Bedtime, kids," Dad says.

"But Dad, you should see this," I start.

I can hear Jessie beginning to pack up the telescope.

On the roof across the street, the sparks start flying again.

"Squishy," Dad says, but I ignore him, trying to work out what the spacewoman is doing.

"Squishy, if you don't come now, what am I going to say *next* time you ask to do something special?"

I tear myself away, but I've already made a secret promise: I'm *going* to find out who that spacewoman is. Dad can make us go to bed right now, but he doesn't watch us every second of the day.

Chapter Four

"What *was* that?" Vee whispers from the top bunk.

Vee, Jessie and I are lying in our triple bunk bed in the dark, with me in the middle bunk.

"It was a whole meteor shower," Jessie says dreamily from the bottom bunk. She doesn't seem to care that she didn't see the meteor shower through the telescope.

I try to bring her back to reality. "Jessie, there was a spacewoman on the roof, and you didn't even look."

"There was *not* a spacewoman," Jessie says.

"There was so," Vee insists. "With sparks flying everywhere. We both saw it. Squishy's not making things up."

Jessie snorts like she doesn't believe anything.

"Seriously, Jessie," I say, using my most serious voice. "It's true." I roll over and crane my neck, looking out of our window to the building next to Boring Lady's. "The spacewoman was right . . . *there.*"

Our bunk bed creaks as Jessie and Vee roll over and try to look.

The spacewoman's floor is one above ours, so you can't actually see the roof. Just then, a **fountain of sparks** shoots out, right where we're looking. Jessie and Vee squeal.

I cheer as if it's fireworks and say, "I told you. I *told* you. Didn't I tell you?"

Our bedroom door slams open, and Alice is standing there. "That is *enough*!" she growls.

I open my mouth. "But there's an astro–"

"Astro-*nothing*, Squishy," Alice snaps. "Not another *peep*. It's *late,* and you've got school tomorrow."

Alice is being super unfair because she likes her own kids better than me. I wasn't the only one looking at the astronaut. But there's no point trying to tell stuff to grown-ups who are that grumpy. As soon as she closes the door, we all creep out of bed and stand by the window where the telescope usually is.

"Can we set up the telescope?" Vee whispers to Jessie.

Jessie shakes her head. "I left it in the living room, and it's so heavy and clunky. They'd definitely hear us."

The sparks fly again, and Jessie grips my arm. Vee shuffles closer, and I'm tingling as if the sparks are inside me.

Weird stuff like this is the best.

I wake up with Baby on my head. Vee has put him on my pillow and is laughing at us both. Baby **swings** at my face and dribbles on my cheek. He's got smushed food down his little T-shirt.

"Ugh," I say. "You're gross, Baby!"

Then I snuffle my nose in the soft skin under his ear. He giggles. Our Baby has the cutest giggle in the universe. I take him into the kitchen and get us both some breakfast.

I'm so hungry that I eat a bowl of yoghurt with banana slices and honey, five pieces of toast and a chocolate chip cookie I find on the sofa. Baby eats my toast crusts and smears most of a banana on his legs. I'm still in my pyjamas and so is Vee. I feel like last night's excitement is still hanging in the air.

"Mum?" Vee asks. "Do any astronauts live in our city?"

Alice is eating toast, packing her bag, and checking her phone at the same time. "Um, probably."

"Is the space station really two hundred and forty-nine miles away?" I ask.

Alice nods with a mouthful of toast.

Jessie sits down at the table. Her neat ponytail swings shinily. She does her I-told-you-so face.

Vee still isn't convinced. "But Mum, that means the space station is closer than England is to Switzerland!" she says.

Even Dad turns around from where he's making our packed lunches. "Are you being serious, Al?"

Alice laughs, swinging her bag onto her shoulder. "Yep. If there was a road, you could cycle there in a weekend."

Dad smiles, sort of **blushing**. His other cycling friends are faster than him. "Maybe a *long* weekend."

Alice is a lecturer of astrophysics. Mostly that means she does maths. But it also means she brought home our telescope when the university got better ones. And she knows things about astronauts.

"But why would there be a spacewoman on the roof?" I ask.

"What roof?" Alice asks.

"The one across the . . ." I start to point, and then Alice notices something.

"Squishy Taylor, are you still in your pyjamas?"

I look around. "Vee is too," I say. Because being the bad one by yourself is the worst.

"It's ten minutes till **blast-off** to school, kiddo!" Alice says, ignoring Vee. "Get a move on."

She kisses Dad, grinning up at him. "Good luck getting them out the door," she says. "Have a good day, everyone." But she doesn't smile at me.

Baby bounces on Dad's hip as we run to the bus stop. We just miss the bus and stand there, watching it go up the hill. It's six minutes until the next one. We'll miss the first bell, but we won't be *very* late.

Our bus stop is two buildings away from where we live. Across the road from us is where we saw the spacewoman. I lean against the bus stop, looking up at the spacewoman's building. It's just apartments with a car park in the basement. It looks a lot like where we live.

"You know what?" I whisper to Vee. "I bet we could get up to that roof."

Chapter Five

At school I try to do the maths problems our teacher gives us, because astronauts have to be good at maths, but the numbers don't make sense. At break time I do a flip off the monkey bars and land funny on my leg. It doesn't even hurt that badly, but it reminds me about not being able to hug my mum. After lunch I fall asleep on my notebook and wake up in a **puddle of drool**. I feel yucky, and I'm mad at my friends for not waking me up, even though they're nice about the drool.

On the bus home, Jessie and Vee and I all sit together on one seat.

"So," Vee says, "how would we get to the spacewoman's roof?"

Jessie swishes her ponytail. "There *is* no spacewoman," she says.

"What were those sparks, then?" I ask.

Jessie shrugs. "I don't know. Some kind of machinery, I suppose."

"Yeah, like a **rocket**," I say.

Jessie snorts and gets out her book.

"So we need to sneak in," I say.

"We need to follow someone who has a swipe card for the front door," Vee says.

I nod. "Yeah, then race up the fire-escape stairs."

We plan how to spy on the astronaut all the way home, and Jessie ignores us.

As we arrive at our apartment and walk into our kitchen, Jessie says, "You're being idiots. There *is no spacewoman*. It's like Squishy thinking the moon can come in between Earth and a space station. It's ridiculous."

Usually I don't really care that Jessie's so annoying. But right now, all the bad things in my day are hurting my chest.

"Ugh," I growl. "Jessie, do you have to be so **serious**? It's like you *want* to miss out on all the good stuff. You want the world to be as boring as you are. Well, it's not. There's weird stuff happening, Jessie. We saw it. You're just being like this to make yourself look better than us."

I drop my bag in the middle of the floor with a bang.

"Who didn't get enough sleep last night?" Dad asks, with his most smug smile. I hate it when I'm **furious** and grown-ups tell me it's because I'm tired.

Dad makes us smoothies, which is good. But he decides to walk to the playground with us, which is bad. It means we can't scope out the building across the road.

I try to get Dad to do astronaut training on the space station with us. But he can't do that and hold Baby at the same time. He ends up with Jessie, turning the solar system around instead. They both talk seriously, as if there isn't supposed to be fun in the universe *ever*. When there's a mystery somewhere else, the playground is just stupid.

After dinner I Skype Mum. I tell her all the **stupid-rubbish-bad** things that happened in my day.

She says, "Oh, Squishy-sweet, I wish I could give you a big hug."

I remember what it used to be like, with my head under her chin and her arms tight around me. We used to cuddle every single day of my life (except on Dad weekends). But now she's so far away.

I think of something. "Did you know that Geneva is further away from London than the space station?"

Mum grins. "Someone has been paying attention in geography lessons!" she says.

I glance out of our bedroom window and gasp. The sparks are showering on the roof again.

I say, "Love you, Mum. Gotta go."

Mum smiles. "Well, that was sudden. Love you too!"

I turn off Skype and sit up.

"Vee! Jessie! Come in here!" I call. "Jessie, bring the telescope."

"Bed in three minutes!" Dad shouts.

Jessie and Vee run in and push their faces against the glass.

"Again," Vee says.

Jessie pulls the telescope and tripod out. She's good at putting things together. When Alice built our bunk beds, Vee helped me carry everything up from the car. Then we got bored and played with Baby. But Jessie measured wood and marked screw holes and did bolting with Alice for two entire days.

Jessie sets up the telescope super fast. But there's not really anything to see. Our floor is too low. The sparks are clearer, but that's about it.

"It's just some type of machinery," Jessie says.

"Yeah, but if it's not a rocket, *what is it*?" Vee asks.

Jessie bites her lip and shakes her head, still watching the sparks. I can tell she's interested.

"We need to get out on the roof again," I say.

"Well, Tom forgot to give the roof key back," Jessie says. "It's still on the table by the door."

Nice work, Dad, I think.

Chapter Six

After Dad says good night, I fall asleep straight away, but Jessie's alarm wakes us up.

"It's ten o'clock," Jessie says. "They should be asleep now. Let's go."

We tiptoe through the kitchen. Jessie has the telescope, Vee has the tripod, and I take the keys from the table. We're like **ninja-shadows** in the corridor and up the stairs.

When we reach the roof, I prop the door open with a handy brick, so we don't get locked out up here.

There are no sparks, and for a second I'm disappointed. But the rocket shape is still there.

"Look," Vee says. "What's that?"

I see a dark shadow moving around the rocket.

Jessie's setting up the telescope in record time and focusing on the shadow. "What's she *doing*?" she says, almost to herself.

I hop from foot to foot beside her, wanting a turn at the telescope. Vee keeps glancing from Jessie to the rocket and back again.

"What is it, Jessie? Is it a rocket?" I ask. "Why is she building a rocket?"

"It's hard to tell what it is," Jessie says. "She's covering it up with something – a big sheet of plastic, I think."

"Because she doesn't want people to see it when the sun comes up," I say. "She's hiding something. Something big!"

Vee is nodding. "Exactly. That's why she has to work secretly, at night."

We take turns watching the red-haired woman as she ties the plastic over her rocket and puts away her tools.

"Do you think she's some kind of **renegade astronaut?**" I ask.

Vee looks away from the telescope. "Why else would someone build a rocket?" she asks.

"Maybe she's an alien just trying to find her way back home," I suggest, and I'm only half-joking. Maybe she *is* an alien.

Jessie **snorts**. "It's not a rocket. Real rockets are much bigger than that."

"Yeah, but even *you* don't know how big an alien rocket is," I say. Which is totally true, but Jessie doesn't think I've won the argument. She snorts again.

Vee pulls away from the telescope again. "Whatever she is, she's gone," she says.

We pack up slowly and head back downstairs.

When we get to our door, I'm just putting the key into the lock when Jessie's eyes widen and she grabs my hand to stop me. She puts her ear to the door and waves us to do the same. On the other side I hear the muffled sound of Baby crying and Alice walking back and forth in the kitchen.

That was close! Now we're stuck out here until Baby goes back to sleep.

"Phew," Jessie says. "Let's hope she doesn't check our room."

We slide down against the door.

"I want to go to bed," Vee whispers.

I nod. I'm suddenly really tired. I'm desperate to be in my bed. I almost think we should just open the door and face getting into trouble. But I can't even be bothered to stand up, so I close my eyes.

I wake up with Vee shaking me. My neck feels stiff, and my back is sore where it's been leaning against the door.

"Get up," Vee says. "Get up. We fell asleep. It's morning."

The corridor has grey, early morning light that's coming in from the window at the fire-escape end.

Jessie pushes her ear against the door and then shakes her head. "They're not up yet. **Lucky**. OK, we just have to get ourselves into the bedroom before they open their door."

I ease the key into the lock. "Quietly," Jessie says. "*Quietly*."

I place the keys as gently as I can on the table and tiptoe across the kitchen after the others. We close our bedroom door, scramble into our bunks, and burst into a fit of muffled giggles.

"We slept in the corridor half the night!" I whisper.

"I can't believe we just did that," Jessie says.

"How long till breakfast?" Vee asks.

"Who cares about breakfast?" I say, remembering what we saw last night. "We *have* to find out more about the rocket."

Chapter Seven

Somehow I fall back asleep.

When I wake up, Jessie is rummaging with something right next to my head.

"Whaaa . . . ?" I ask sleepily, rolling over to see what she's doing.

Jessie has stuck the iPad onto the telescope with sticky tape. Then she taps open the iPad camera app and tilts the telescope down towards the street below.

"What are you *doing*?" I ask, more awake now.

"Breakfast is ready!" Dad calls from the kitchen. Then Baby starts crying.

But I'm staring at Jessie's new device. She's filming *through* the telescope. And the telescope is focused on the front door of Spacewoman's building.

"Genius," I whisper.

"It's our own spy camera. Now we can see every time she comes and goes from the building."

"That's *so cool*, Jess," Vee says, from her bunk.

Jessie nods, a bit smugly. "Yep. I've even plugged the iPad in to charge so it doesn't run out of battery while we're at school."

"Jessie, you are the **best bonus sister ever**," I say.

"I'm calling it a tele-pad," Jessie says, and I grin.

Dad calls from the kitchen again. "If you're not up in fifteen seconds, this bucket of ice-water is going over your heads!"

He'd never do that. But it makes us laugh, and we climb, jump, flip and scramble out of bed.

"We want to learn her habits," Jessie says as the bus rumbles us to school. "When does she usually leave the building? When does she come home? What does she carry? Stuff like that."

I squirm in the seat. I can't wait to get home and find out what our new spy camera has filmed.

"I bet she carries wiring and computers and satellites," Vee says.

"Yeah, and **special alien food** and letters for the president of the galaxy," I add.

The others laugh. The president of the galaxy is from *Lightspeed Kids,* and we all know he's not real.

"I wish we didn't have to go to school," Vee says.

I almost agree. But there's one reason I *do* want to go to school. "If we want to be astronauts, we need to get good at maths," I say.

Vee groans. Jessie laughs. Jessie's already good at maths.

When we get home, we rush to the tele-pad. At first I lean in close, watching every second. But there's nothing for a while. It turns out watching the whole day go by is really boring, even in fast forward. Vee and I take turns practising bunk-bed tricks and looking over Jessie's shoulder.

Nothing happens in real life or in the video, except for people going in and out. None of them are Spacewoman. I'm starting to feel pretty disappointed. Then I realize something.

"That's weird," I say. "Spacewoman *never* leaves the building."

Jessie shakes her head. "She could have left for work before I set it up and not be home yet. We just have to wait a bit longer."

I don't want to wait.

Jessie sets up the tele-pad again. "The cool thing about the tele-pad is that it does the waiting for us, and we can do other things."

"Why don't we just sneak up to her roof?" I ask.

Vee does a **rolling-spin-drop** from her bunk. "That would be more fun than waiting to see what's on a camera."

Jessie doesn't look convinced, but she steps away from the telescope.

We stride out of our front door and cross at the lights near Spacewoman's building. It has an entrance hall just like ours, with glass doors that need a swipe card.

We watch a few people swipe and open the doors.

"OK," I say. "Next person who comes, we follow them in."

The next person to step up to the door is a tired-looking man wearing silly blue pyjamas and trainers.

"Why is he wearing pyjamas?" Vee whispers.

"Shhh," I say, and squeeze her arm.

As the tired man steps through the door, I jump forward to catch it and keep it open.

We're in.

Chapter Eight

We wait by the lift with the man in blue pyjamas. I hope he doesn't notice that we don't have our own swipe card. Luckily he's scrolling through his phone and barely even glances at us.

We follow him into the lift, and Vee nudges my arm, nodding at his pyjamas. I try not to laugh. Jessie frowns at us. At the ninth floor, the lift stops, and we follow Pyjama Man out. He goes right to the door by the lift and digs in his pocket for his keys. Where to now?

Jessie spots the fire-escape door at the end of the corridor and leads the way. As soon as we reach the stairs and the door closes behind us, our giggles burst out.

"We made it!" I say. We **high-five** each other.

"That man was wearing pyjamas," Jessie says in the same tone she uses when she discovers a new fact on the internet.

"In *public*," Vee says. "Why was he wearing pyjamas in public?"

I start running up the stairs. "No idea," I say. "Let's go and find a rocket."

Vee and Jessie chase me up the stairs. My astronaut training has paid off. I can run even faster than I used to, and Vee is right behind. Jessie is slower, but we're all at the top pretty soon. The door to the roof is different from the one in our building. There's no gate, and the stairs go all the way up. The door looks as though people open it all the time.

There is a sign. "Residents and guests only," Jessie reads aloud.

"I laugh in the face of residents," I say, pushing open the door. It's like our favourite line from *Lightspeed Kids*, but funny because I changed it from *enemies* to *residents*.

Vee snorts and laughs. "Especially when the residents wear pyjamas," she says.

I step out onto the roof and into a garden. Someone's growing vegetables and flowers up here. It's like our balcony times a million. So many pots and tubs and wooden boxes full of plants.

"Dad would love this," I say. Dad's job is making other people's gardens good. He has all these books about gardens that people grow in strange places.

"Hey, look," Vee says. "**Strawberries!**" They're still green but so cute, tucked in under their leaves.

Then I remember to look for the rocket. It's on the other side of the roof. In between it and us is a tall wire fence.

The rocket is covered with a huge piece of blue plastic.

"It does look rocket-shaped," Jessie admits from where we're standing with our faces pushed up against the wire.

"But you can't actually see what's underneath."

I pull back, looking for a way in. The fence has a gate with a padlock.

I can do the hairpin trick on most padlocks.

"Anyone got a hairpin?" I ask.

Jessie and Vee shake their heads.

"Hi there," says a voice behind us. We jump. It's Pyjama Man, but he's not wearing pyjamas any more. He's wearing jeans and a T-shirt like Dad wears.

I gulp. **Busted.**

"Um, hello," Jessie says to Pyjama Man, who's carrying a glass of fizzy water with a slice of lemon in it.

Vee pinches me and whispers, "Don't look so guilty."

"Hi!" I say brightly, doing my smile-and-look-them-in-the-eye thing. Mum would be proud.

"I've never seen you kids here before," he says. "What are you up to?"

My heart beats faster. Quick! Make something up. "Um, we're visiting our, um, cousin," I say. "He lives downstairs."

"Actually we should probably see how he's doing," Jessie says, turning towards the door.

Pyjama Man sits on a wooden chair and leans back with a sigh.

I'm following Jessie, but Vee doesn't move.

"Why were you wearing pyjamas?" she asks him.

I stop to see what he says.

He looks confused, then laughs. "Oh, you mean my scrubs? I'm a nurse. That's my uniform."

Scrubs? Uniform for nurses? Then I imagine him with a white face mask standing next to a hospital bed. He's right. Nurses wear pyjamas. I've seen it on TV.

The man sips his drink while Vee stares at him. Then he asks, "Is your cousin that cute kid who lives on the fifth floor?"

"Yes," says Vee.

"No," Jessie says, at the same time.

The man raises his eyebrows. Jessie and Vee look really guilty.

Squishy Taylor to the rescue. "Our cousin does live on the fifth floor," I say, "but he's not cute. He's **gross**."

We have to get out of here before

Pyjama Man asks any more tricky questions.

I grab Vee's hand and pull her out the door. We tumble down the stairs and head home.

Vee looks a little disappointed. "We didn't see the rocket," she says.

I don't really mind. "That's OK," I say. "Now we know the way to the roof for next time."

Chapter Nine

That evening Jessie interrupts my Skype session with Mum on the sofa.

"Sorry, Devika. I need Squishy," she says, pulling at my shoulder.

"Bye, Mum!" I call.

Jessie pulls me into our room. The sparks have started again – showering off the roof across the road. We huddle around Vee, who's already watching at the window.

"We need to get up there *now*," Vee says, "while she's making the sparks."

I nod. And then shake my head. "Dad and Alice will never let us."

"You're right," Jessie says. "And you know what? We don't actually need to be there to find things out. What do we already *know* about her?"

Jessie gets her notebook and felt-tip pens (in perfect rainbow order), and we sprawl on our bedroom floor together. I lean my chin on my hands, watching her write.

- She makes sparks.

- The sparks happen between dinnertime and 10 o'clock.

- She hides what she's doing.

"She's a spacewoman," I say.

Jessie groans. "Squishy, she's *not* a spacewoman."

I grin. "OK, maybe an alien."

Jessie hits my shoulder with her pen.

"**Ow**," I say and then get serious. "But she *was* wearing an astronaut's helmet that first night, wasn't she, Vee?"

Vee nods, so Jessie writes:

- She wears a form of protective helmet.

This is the thing about Jessie. Just when you think she's fun, she starts using boring grown-up words.

"What else?" Jessie asks.

"I wish we could get out *while she's working*," I say, looking over at the sparks flying in the night.

But between dinner and 10 o'clock is the hardest time to sneak away from Dad and Alice.

On Friday, Saturday and Sunday, we keep a close eye on the building whenever we can. Jessie scans the tele-pad every night before bed. Once it's dark, the camera app doesn't really record very much. Jessie scrolls through the footage she's taken from dawn till dark every day.

Spacewoman never leaves the building.

We see Pyjama Man lots of times, going in and out in his pyjamas. But we never see a red-headed spacewoman.

Even at the weekend. And yet some nights we still see sparks on the roof.

Every day it gets creepier and creepier. We *have* to find out what she's doing.

It's not until Monday night that Dad and Alice go to bed early enough for us to sneak out.

"Shh," I say with my ear against our bedroom door. "I think they're in bed."

We wait a few more minutes and then crack open the door.

My rucksack is on the kitchen floor. I take a big step over it, and Jessie follows. Behind me there's a noise. I turn to see Vee, who has tripped over the rucksack. She bumps into the worktop and knocks the frying pan into a mug, which falls and smashes on the tiled floor.

Three seconds of **horror** later, Alice flicks on the light. "*What* is going *on*?"

"Um, we were just–" I start.

But Alice doesn't let me finish. "Squishy Taylor, why are you even *talking* right now?"

"You asked us a question," I say. Which is a perfectly reasonable answer.

Sometimes Alice can be really sarcastic. "Well, I'm sorry for *confusing* you," she says in a super-mean voice. Then she snaps, "What I meant was, *go to bed*. This very second."

"Well you should have *said* that," I say sulkily.

"Stop talking right now, Squishy," Alice says, gripping my shoulder with sharp fingers and pointing me to the bedroom.

Why is she being horrible to me and not the others? But as soon as I turn around, I realize they've already gone to bed. I suppose they already know how mean their mum is.

I bite down on all the things I want to shout at Alice and scramble into my bunk.

She practically slams the door.

"No point trying to sneak out again tonight," Vee whispers.

I can still feel Alice's fingers where they held my shoulder. I know we were officially in the wrong, but I'm mad at her for aiming all her **anger** at me.

Jessie whispers, "The problem is that Mum and Tom are too wide awake when we need them to be asleep."

Vee starts talking, and I can hear a grin in her voice. "We should tire them out so they go to bed really early."

We make a new plan. Alice is going to hate it. It's genius.

The next night, we drag out going to bed as late as we possibly can. I brush my teeth for about half an hour. Vee spills milk in her bunk and needs to have her sheets changed. Jessie claims she forgot to practise violin, and Alice lets her stay up. (They'd probably let her practise violin at three in the morning if she wanted to.)

Then, just before finally going to bed, I sneak some red juice into Baby's sippy-cup and hand it over. He grabs it with his fat little hands and starts **slurping.**

By the time they kiss us goodnight, it's *way* past bedtime. And that's only the beginning.

Vee is first. Twenty minutes after Dad and Alice's bedroom door closes, she scrambles down. We listen to her whine, "Muuuum, I'm still awaaaake."

Alice grumbles but brings her back to bed.

We let ourselves go to sleep because Jessie has set an alarm.

I wake up to hear Jessie screaming, "Eeeeeeek! Spider, spider! Help!"

A minute later, Dad flicks on the light.

"There! Spider! Eeeek!" says Jessie.

Dad runs around the room with a plastic container, but he can't find the "spider".

Jessie is actually a really good actor. She makes him crawl under the bed and pull off all her covers and shake them before she finally agrees to go back to bed. When Dad leaves, we high-five each other over the edges of our beds, giggling quietly.

Mine is the best job. At four in the morning, the alarm goes off. It's still dark, and I tiptoe as quietly as I can to the kitchen for a cup of warm water. I take the cup into Dad and Alice's room where Baby is in his cot by the door. This is the trickiest part. Can I wake up Baby without being caught?

I pull back his blankets, pour the water all over his nappy and legs, give his tummy a little poke for good measure, and then hurry out of the room.

I wait. Did it work?

"Waaaaaaah!"

Perfect. Now he'll be awake until breakfast time. A job well done. Dad and Alice will go to bed super early tomorrow, and we can finally get a good look at Spacewoman's rocket. I slip back to sleep.

Chapter Ten

We were totally right. Alice and Dad go to bed at 8.38 p.m., which is pretty much a record.

We pull on our coats and shoes and tiptoe out the door to the lift. We have to get across the street without being noticed by a grown-up who thinks they can tell us what to do. It's all about looking confident – like we know exactly where we're going. But not so confident that people think we're **hooligans**. (An old woman called us **hooligans** once when we were having too much fun on the bus.)

It's not far. Just up to the traffic lights and across the street. No one pays any attention to us. We pause on the pavement in front of Spacewoman's apartment building. We can't open the front door ourselves.

"Now we wait," I say. "Someone will go in soon."

But nobody comes.

We stand by the door forever. It's hard to look confident but not like a **hooligan** when you're just hanging around on the pavement way after bedtime. A couple walks past and makes stern faces, as if we're doing something naughty. If it was daytime, we could play hopscotch and no one would even notice us.

A man walks towards us. I think maybe this is our chance. He's about to go through the front door. But he doesn't. He stops in front of us.

"You kids all right?" he asks.

"We're fine," I say.

He looks at us, waiting for me to say something else.

I glance at Jessie. She looks so guilty, it's like she just killed a puppy.

"We're just waiting for our . . . um . . . cousin," Vee says. "He lives up there."

The man shrugs. "OK. As long as you're not in trouble?"

"We're fine," I say again.

He walks away slowly and looks over his shoulder at us a couple of times.

"We've gotta get inside," Vee says.

"But *how*?" I ask.

Jessie comes to the rescue. "I've got a plan," she says. "Let's hope this works."

I watch her step up and press the buzzer. "Who are you calling?" I ask.

"Hello?" a voice comes out of the speaker.

"Hey," Jessie says. "My name's Jessie, I'm one of the kids you met on the roof the other day?"

"Ye-es?" the man says, uncertainly.

"**Pyjama Man?**" I whisper, and Jessie puts her finger to her lips and nods.

"Remember how we were visiting our cousin last time?" Jessie asks. "Well, it's his birthday today. We really want to surprise him before bedtime. Could you please let us in?"

"Um, I suppose so."

There's a pause, and then the door buzzes. We're inside.

"Jessie you're a genius!" I say, high-fiving her.

"That was awesome. How did you know his number?" Vee asks.

Jessie smirks. "I was looking when he unlocked his door. It just stayed in my memory. I sort of forgot about it until now."

We get in the lift up to the ninth floor and then jog up the stairs.

I turn back towards the others as I reach the rooftop access door. "Now shhhh, Spacewoman is probably there already."

"She's not a spacewoman," Jessie hisses.

I push open the door and tiptoe out onto the roof with the others behind me. We have to be super careful. Spacewoman only works at night and never leaves her building. She is officially really creepy and might be an **alien**. Who knows what she does to kids who spy on her? I start to feel a little scared but also excited.

There's a light on over by Spacewoman's rocket but no sparks. She's probably there, working away, getting ready to fly into space. We creep over towards her fence. Yes! The gate is unlocked. And the rocket is uncovered.

Jessie gasps, and I grin in the dark.

It *is* a rocket. A real-life metal rocket, taller than my dad.

Vee is squeezing my arm, and I've got my face pressed up against the wires.

"Is Spacewoman there?" Vee whispers.

I can't see her.

There's a lamp on over a workbench with some tools on it. Next to the rocket is a cylinder, which looks like a massive oxygen tank. The space helmet is resting on the worktop. It's dark green with a tinted window. But there's no Spacewoman.

"I don't think she's there," I say, moving closer to the gate. Vee and Jessie stay close beside me.

Without the fence in front of it, the rocket is **beautiful**. The silvery metal

shines in the city lights. I can't help walking towards it to take a closer look.

"Squishy, what are you doing?" Jessie whispers.

"Squishy, she'll catch you," Vee hisses. I can hear her nervousness.

I peep around the back of the rocket.

"It's OK, she's not here," I call.

I wonder where she is. Then I turn and look at the rocket again. It's just perfect for flying into another galaxy, though it's not quite finished. The three fins bend out at the base beautifully. It has a door with four little steps going up to it, and the rocket is covered all around in a skin of shining curved metal. But a strip of the covering along the bottom is missing. You can still see the skeleton frame.

I realize something as Jessie and Vee join me.

"This rocket is wrong," I say.

Jessie is nodding and opens her mouth like she's about to speak.

But Vee grabs us both at once. "Shhh," she says. "The door–"

The door to the roof creaks open, and we see a rectangle of light appear on the concrete. Then a human shadow moves in the light.

Spacewoman is back.

Chapter Eleven

Spacewoman is coming, but I know exactly what to do.

"**Quick!** Get in," I whisper and lead the way up into the rocket.

We crouch together inside the rocket and hold our breath. Because of the missing strip, if she looks closely she'll see us. Luckily it's still pretty dark on the roof. I cross my fingers. Spacewoman comes towards us but doesn't say anything.

She starts moving things around on the workbench.

As soon as I know she hasn't seen us, I go back to noticing how wrong this rocket is.

"It's way too small," I whisper to Jessie, who's squished in next to me. We still have to be so quiet, because Spacewoman is so close.

"And there's no room for the engine," Vee whispers. I realize she's right. There's barely room for three kids.

Jessie has a tiny smirk on her face. I can just see it in the dark. "And doesn't this metal look sort of familiar?"

It does look familiar. But I can't remember where I've seen it before.

"Shhh." Vee grabs me again.

Spacewoman lifts up a sheet of metal and pushes it so it covers the frame of the spaceship. She's filling in the last strip. It's so close to where my knees are! She pulls on her space helmet, lifts a long metal tube from beside the oxygen tank, and fiddles with something. Then there's a **pop** and a **hiss**. A blue-white flame bursts from the tube.

That's not a space helmet or an oxygen tank.

"She's welding," Jessie whispers.

"What's welding?" Vee asks.

I know the answer to that, but Spacewoman is too close for me to speak out loud. Welding is joining metal by melting it. With a really hot flame.

The flame comes closer and closer to my knee. We try to shift away from it, but there's no room. The flame is so close that I can feel the heat. Sparks start to fly off the rocket. I can't stay here any more. I don't care that Spacewoman will find out we're here.

Better busted than dead.

"STOP!" I shout.

Spacewoman screams and leaps backwards. She drags the flame-tube with her. The oxygen tank falls over with a big bang. Spacewoman tumbles backwards onto the ground and lets the flame-tube go. Fire is shooting out of the tube sideways towards the wooden workbench.

We hurry out of the rocket.

Spacewoman is gasping and struggling to stand up and get hold of the fire-tube. The flame is worming everywhere. Her helmet looks really heavy, and I can tell she needs help. I run towards her.

"Squishy, no!" calls Jessie.

Spacewoman says, "Stop, stay clear."

She doesn't know how super strong I am. I reach my hand out to help her up.

And the fire-tube twists and fire shoots straight at my wrist.

I stare as the flame hits my skin, but I can't feel anything. There's just this hissing silence. Then I scream. Spacewoman screams. Vee screams.

And Jessie turns off the fire. She's crouching by a twisty knob at the tank. "Are you OK, Squishy?"

The burning feeling starts. It stings so horribly.

"**Ow, ow, ow!**" I want to clutch my wrist, but I'm scared to touch it. I feel **panicky**, and it **hurts**.

Spacewoman has suddenly got over her shock. She whips off her helmet, lifts me up, and runs me over to the wall at the edge of the building. There's a tap sticking out at hip height. She drops me to my feet, turns the water on full force and shoves my arm under it.

I'm crying.

Jessie and Vee run up beside us. I don't even try to stop crying.

"What were you kids *doing*?" asks Spacewoman, easing the tap so the water runs more softly.

"Is it really bad, Squishy?" Vee asks.

Jessie has turned into the responsible older sister all of a sudden. "Vee, go and get Mum, quickly. I'll stay with Squishy."

"OK." Vee doesn't even pause. She sprints for the door.

Chapter Twelve

As the door closes behind Vee, I realize something. I don't want her to get Alice. I want her to get **Dad**. All I want is a big cuddle on his knee. And Alice was so horrible last night. But it's too late.

Spacewoman holds my arm under the water, saying things like, "What were you *thinking*? Good grief! How did you even get up here?"

Jessie turns the lamp around and brings it closer, until it's at the end of its cord.

"Good thinking," says Spacewoman. "Thanks."

I sit there, watching the water trickle over my burned, sore arm and run down the drain.

The door finally opens. I was hoping Vee would realize I needed Dad, but she didn't. It's Alice, with Vee right behind her. Alice looks sleepy, horrified, embarrassed and anxious all at the same time. I wait for her to shout at me.

She doesn't.

She runs over, kneels down and gently takes my elbow, trying to see the burn in the lamplight. "Oh, Squishy – **jeepers!** What have you kids been *doing*?"

She turns to Spacewoman. "I'm so sorry about all this. You must be shocked. They're not usually like this." She pauses. "Well, actually they are, but they're good kids, really. Oh, what am I even *saying*?"

Alice turns back to me and pulls me onto her lap. She's really careful not to pull my arm out from under the running water. "Squishy, does it hurt?" She leans her face in next to mine to look down at the burn. Her arms hold me tight.

Her cheek feels soft and friendly. It's not like Mum. And it's not like Dad. It's Alice. But it's Alice in a new, **comfortable** way that makes me feel safe. I lean back into her and cry a little bit more.

Someone else steps out onto the roof.

"Is everyone OK up here?"

It's Pyjama Man.

"Hey, Rasheed," Spacewoman says.

"Hey!" Pyjama Man grins. "Nice to see you at home, rather than at work." He looks around at all of us. "I just had my *second* strange doorbell ring this evening–"

Vee smiles sideways at Jessie and whispers, "Lucky I still remembered his apartment number, otherwise we wouldn't have got back in."

Pyjama Man is still talking. "–and I got worried about what was going on up here." He looks down at my arm under the tap. "A burn? Not too terrible, I see. And you've got the best nurse in the burns ward looking after you too."

He winks at Spacewoman, and I turn in Alice's lap and stare.

"You're a nurse? Not a spacewoman?" I ask.

Spacewoman glances over at her **space helmet** and then smiles at me. "Yes, I am a nurse. And in fact, it's almost time for me to go to work. Maybe we should go to the hospital together?" She glances at Alice, who nods.

"Cool!" says Vee, looking interestedly at my arm. "You're *so* injured you have to go to the hospital."

But Jessie isn't paying attention to Vee or my arm. She's staring at Spacewoman like she's just realized something. "You work the *night shift*!" she says.

Spacewoman nods.

Jessie grins. "So you leave for work now, and you get home at . . . ?"

"Five-thirty in the morning," says the spacewoman.

"Oh," I say. I get it. I lean back into Alice. No wonder we never saw Spacewoman go through the front door. "You only go out when it's dark!"

Spacewoman nods as if she doesn't understand why we're so interested and then turns to put away her tools.

Alice and Pyjama Man start talking about how long it takes to walk to the hospital (not long), and Vee starts begging to come too. I watch the water run over my arm, thinking hard. How can she be a nurse if she's building a rocket?

Chapter Thirteen

Spacewoman meets us on the street in her **nurse-pyjamas**. Vee and Jessie are here too because they begged and because Alice and I didn't have time to walk them home.

"Do you think she's *really* a nurse?" I whisper to Vee as we set off walking under the streetlights to the hospital. Vee shrugs. Alice holds my hand softly, keeping me close.

I'm about to ask what nurses have to do with rockets, but Alice cuts me off. "Now," she says, "I think you three have some explaining to do."

So, as we walk, Jessie tells the story of the sparks on the roof and Vee seeing Spacewoman for the first time. She describes the tele-pad and how I thought Spacewoman was an **alien**.

My arm starts hurting from not being under the water.

Vee explains about making friends with Pyjama Man and how we were going to do the **hairpin trick** on the padlock. The adults shake their heads, but I can tell they're secretly smiling.

The hospital is huge, with enormous glass doors and a shiny tiled floor in the entrance. It's pretty empty at this time of night.

"Look at those *floors*!" says Vee, and she does a **drop-from-running knee-slide**. She goes about five metres before she bumps into a sofa.

"Veronica! Stop it!" Alice calls, and her hand tightens in mine.

But Spacewoman just laughs. "This way," she says. "The kids can wait in here while we grab the paperwork."

Spacewoman takes us to a little room with a tall bed in the middle. Then they leave us there. Everything is so blue and white and shiny. It almost feels like we could be in an actual spaceship.

I sit on the bed.

Vee says, "Hey, look at this!" and presses something on the side. The bed starts going up, up, up, with me on it, and we all laugh.

"How does it work?" Jessie asks, getting in close to look at the switch.

"All signed in," Alice says from the doorway.

Jessie and Vee jump away from the bed, pretending they weren't doing anything. Spacewoman comes in behind Alice, holding a tiny plastic cup.

"This should help with the pain," she says.

I glance at Alice. Should I really take medicine from a rocket builder? But Alice nods, so I drink it. I like how small the cup is.

Spacewoman reaches for my arm. "Now, let's take a look."

I hold out my burn, feeling a bit uncertain. But Spacewoman takes it gently and smooths some cooling cream all over it.

It seems like she really *is* a nurse.

I look up at Spacewoman. "But if you're a nurse, why were you building a rocket?"

"But it's not really a rocket, is it?" Jessie interrupts. "It's for a playground."

As soon as Jessie says it, I realize she's right. The rocket is exactly the right size for playing in, and it's made from the same metal as the space station at our playground. That's why it looked so familiar.

"Did you make the space station and solar system at our park?" I ask.

Spacewoman laughs. "That's me. I'm a sculpture artist. I've got a contract with the city council to make climbable art for playgrounds."

She unwraps a special type of enormous bandage from a packet. It's really thin, and she sticks it carefully along my arm.

"But you're a nurse!" Vee says. "How can you be a sculpture artist?"

"Duh," says Jessie. "She's a nurse *and* a sculpture artist. Just like Mum's an astrophysics lecturer and a bunk-bed builder."

"Not to mention being a **mum** *and* a **bonus mum**," says Alice, winking at me. It makes me remember how comfortable it was sitting on her lap.

I look at Spacewoman. "Is that true? You're a nurse and a rocket-builder? Both?"

Spacewoman grins. "Yep. Sure am. Two completely different jobs. Sometimes it's hard to get work making sculptures, so I don't stop nursing. Besides, I really like fixing people."

She leans back. "All right, brave lady. I think we're all done."

She talks to Alice about how long to keep the bandage on and when to come back to the doctor. My arm has stopped hurting, and I start to feel extra, super sleepy.

"Home time, **Squisho**," I hear Alice say. "You're going to have a lot to tell your mum in the morning."

Then she lifts me up into her arms.

I could walk if I wanted to. I'm probably a bit **big** to be up here. But I'm being held tight, and I feel so comfortable and cosy. So I let Alice carry me all the way home.

THE END

About the author and illustrator

Ailsa Wild is an acrobat, whip-cracker and teaching artist who ran away from the circus to become a writer. She taught Squishy all her best bunk-bed tricks.

Ben Wood started drawing when he was Baby's age and happily drew all over his mum and dad's walls! Since then, he has never stopped drawing. He has an identical twin, and they used to play all kinds of pranks on their younger brother.

Author acknowledgements

Christy and Luke, for writing residencies, bunk-bed acrobatics and the day you turned the truck around.

Antoni, Penni, Moreno and the masterclass crew, for showing me what the journey could be. Here's to epiphanies.

Indira and Devika, because she couldn't be real without you.

Hilary, Marisa, Penny, Sarah and the HGE team, for making it happen. What an amazing net to have landed in.

Ben, for bringing them all to life.

Jono, for independence and supporting each other's dreams.

— Ailsa

Illustrator
acknowledgements

Hilary, Marisa, Sarah and the HGE team, for your enthusiasm and spark.

Penny, for being the best! Thanks for inviting me along on this Squish-tastic ride! (And for putting up with all my emails!)

Ailsa, for creating such a fun place for me to play in.

John, for listening to me ramble on and on about Squishy Taylor every day.

– Ben

Talk about it!

1. What clues does Squishy get that make her think the red-headed woman is an astronaut? Do you think it's fair that Jessie didn't believe her?

2. When Squishy gets hurt towards the end of the story, she wishes she could hug her dad. Have you ever wished you could see a specific person? What made the situation special to that person?

3. Who would you most like to be friends with – Squishy, Jessie or Vee? Talk about your reasons.

Write about it!

1. Squishy and her bonus sisters are put in danger when they lie to their parents, sneak out and hide inside the rocket. Could they have investigated the astronaut in a safer way? Write about another, safer path they could have taken.

2. What do you know about space? Have you ever seen a shooting star? Look up at the night sky. Then write a poem inspired by outer space.

3. Write a get-well card to Squishy. Talk about a time you got hurt and how you knew you were starting to feel better. Illustrate your letter with drawings of spaceships and stars!

For more exciting books from
brilliant authors, check out our website!

www.raintree.co.uk